Dedicated to my wonderful young daughter, Pearl

PEARL POWER

and the Toy Problem

Written and Illustrated by
Mel Elliott

Now Pearl and Sebastian were best of friends.
They weren't at first but they soon made amends.
He started by saying that girls couldn't throw far,
But Pearl showed him

how great little girls are!

And now they would play and act as a team,
and they'd laugh in the sunshine whilst slurping ice cream.
And if anyone said that girls couldn't run fast,
Sebastian would stand there completely aghast.

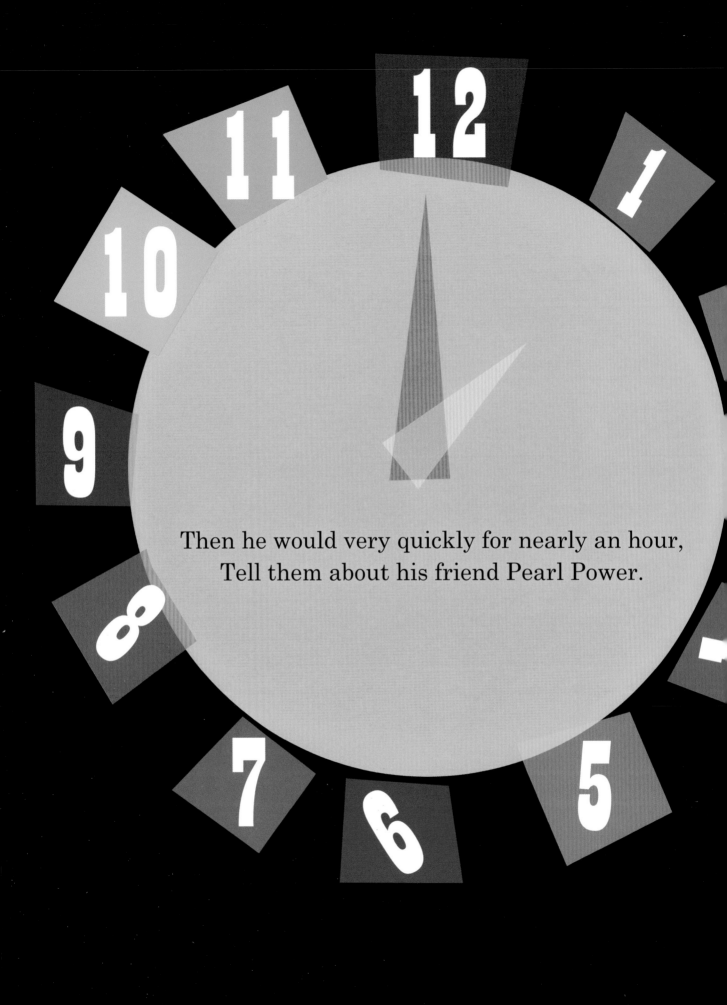

Then he would very quickly for nearly an hour,
Tell them about his friend Pearl Power.

And how she showed him that he was once wrong,
and that both girls and boys are clever and strong.

One day they were playing at Sebastian's home,
there was a knock at the door, it was a boy named Jerome.

Jerome had recently moved in next door,
he had come round to play with his new dinosaur.

Jerome quickly said "You can't play with this Pearl."

"Oh yes of course," Pearl said with a wink
"I'll go and play with that paint as it's pink."

Pearl and Sebastian knew just what to do,
and when Jerome went off to the loo...

They took his T-rex and in a bit of a rush
they painted it pink with the swish of a brush.

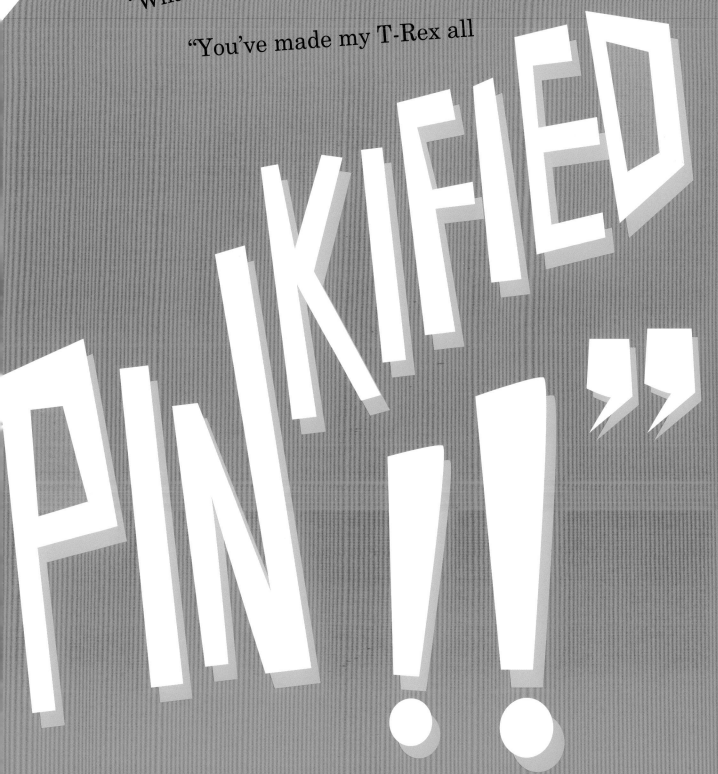

"What have you done!?" Jerome cried,

"You've made my T-Rex all

PINKIFIED!!"

Sebastian calmly explained that toys
such as dinosaurs, aren't just for boys.
And then he told him one thing more
"There's nothing wrong with a pink dinosaur!"

Sebastian and Pearl didn't know what to do,
Jerome had been fooled by the adverts too.

Giving kids rules about toys isn't fun
Toys are for ALL, something had to be done!

"Toy adverts are bad, on this we agree,
so let's write to the woman in charge of TV!"

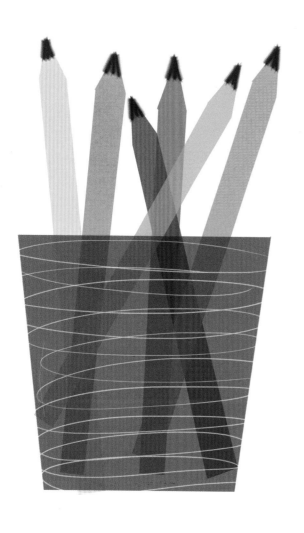

They sat down to write their important letter,
knowing that things could only get better.

They wrote about tractors

and Jerome's dinosaur

and of dolls and of prams

and toy kitchens

and more!

They told her of ponies and pink sparkly purses.
They told her of dressing as doctors and nurses.

And when they had finished in their best handwriting,
they posted their letter, it was really exciting!

doctor

A few days later a letter came through.
Pearl ran to her friend's
"This is *for* me and you!"

Pearl and Seb
Pearl's House
At The Seasi
England

an

They ripped it open as quick as can be,
hoping that someone out there would agree.

Dear Pearl and Sebastian,

Thank you for your letter.
I promise to make adverts
be so much better.
I am sorry to children
in the entire nation,
and I'm banning these adverts
on my TV station!

From now on,
all the makers of toys
will have to stop saying
they're for girls OR for boys.

So boys can have dolls' prams and girls can have trains,
and boys who like sewing will not be called names.
And girls can put boots on and go play football,
and boys can make bracelets, yes, TOYS ARE FOR ALL!

Pearl and Sebastian
jumped up with joy,
and they went to the shop
to buy their favourite toy.

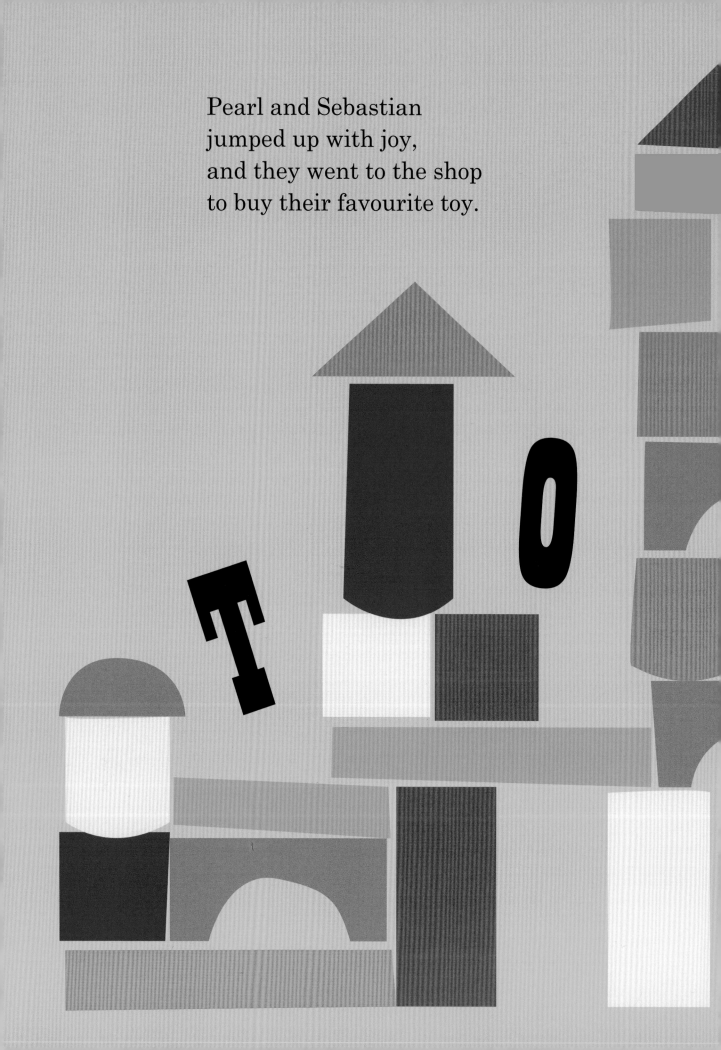

Pearl picked a tool box:
shiny and red.
Sebastian, a teddy,
that would sleep on his bed.

"I know," said Pearl, "let's get one thing more,"

"Let's get Jerome a new dinosaur!"

First published in the United Kingdom by I LOVE MEL
6th Floor, Cavendish House
Hastings
East Sussex
TN34 3AA

I LOVE MEL is a trading name of Brolly Associates Ltd.

ISBN 9780992854485

10 9 8 7 6 5 4 3 2 1

Printed by CMYK, LONDON.

This book can be ordered direct from the publisher at
www.ilovemel.me

Mel Elliott was born in Barnsley, UK and now lives and works in Hastings on the south coast. She is a graduate of The Royal College of Art, London.

Having spent several years illustrating and publishing pop culture colouring books, Mel became inspired by her own daughter, Pearl, and the frustrating issue of gender stereotypes forced upon young children.

Pearl Power and the Toy Problem is the prequel to *Pearl Power* and is Elliott's second book.

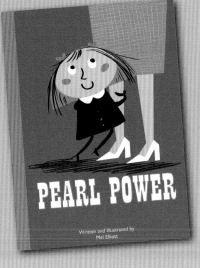

Available from
shop.ilovemel.me